This Orchard book
belongs to

_____

_____

_____

For Anna Barcock
A true friend
With love from Emma

ORCHARD BOOKS

338 Euston Road, London NW1 3BH

Orchard Books Australia

Level 17/207 Kent Street, Sydney, NSW 2000

First published as *I Don't Want a Posh Dog*
in 2008 by Orchard Books
This edition first published in 2014

ISBN 9781408331262

Text © Emma Dodd 2008 & 2014
Illustrations © Emma Dodd 2008 & 2014
The rights of Emma Dodd to be identified as
the author and illustrator of this work has been
asserted by her in accordance with the
Copyright, Designs and Patents Act, 1988.

A CIP catalogue record for this book
is available from the British Library.

1 3 5 7 9 10 8 6 4 2

Printed in China

Orchard Books is a division of Hachette Children's Books,
an Hachette UK company.
www.hachette.co.uk

I love dogs

Emma Dodd

I love
posh dogs,

Blow-dry-when-washed dogs.

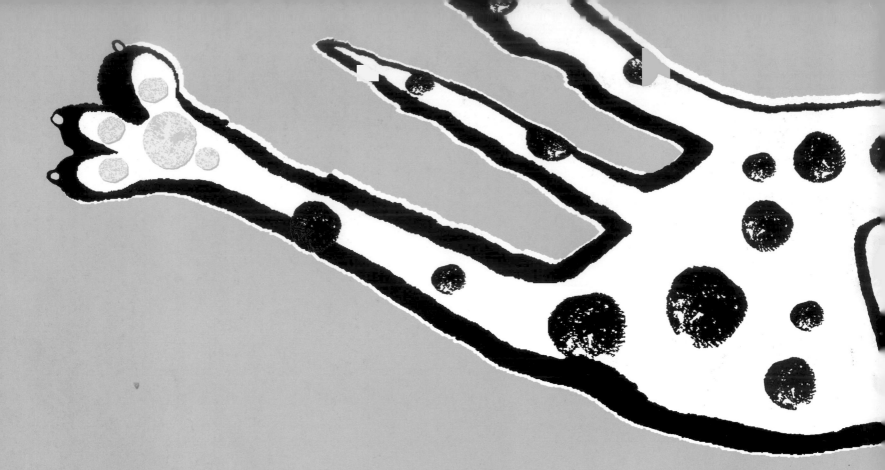

I love
spotty dogs,

Bouncy, jumpy,

dotty dogs.

I love pretty dogs,

Happy-in-the-city dogs.

But I **don't** love
snappy dogs.

Growly,
never-happy
dogs . . .

. . . I **do** love gruff dogs,

Grunty, snuffly, sniff dogs.

And I love

And greedy . . .

. . . weedy,
needy dogs.

I even love
itchy dogs.

Twitchy,

scratchy,

scritchy

dogs.

But my
best dog's
a silly dog.

A sweet, willy-nilly dog.

Not a proud or loud dog.

A know-me-in-the-crowd dog.

An
always-
keen-to-try
dog . . .

. . . a dog I can call

my own dog!

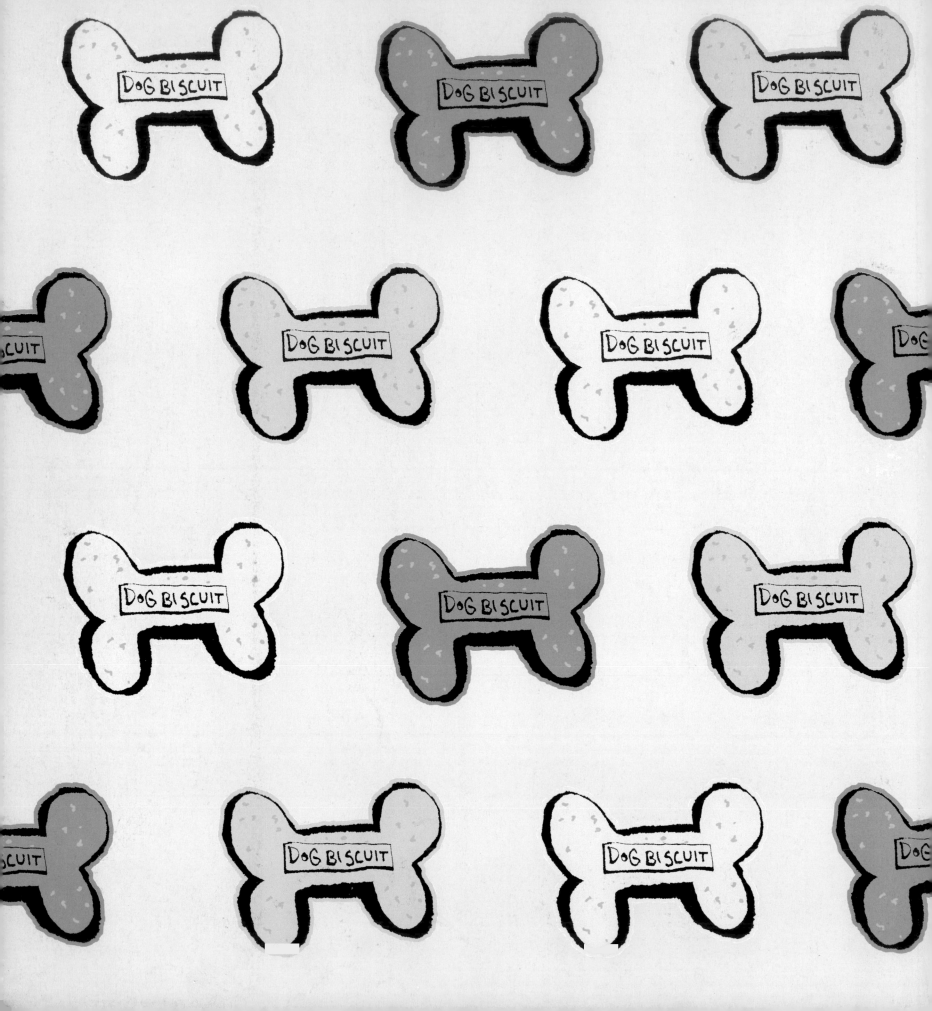